This book belongs to:

....

....

Daddy Dragon
SAVES THE DAY

Printed in the United States of America
First Printing: December, 2019

by Marie Blair
illustrated by
Viktoriia Mykhalevych

In a faraway land where the magic is strong,
And the moon smiles on everyone all night long,
Where goblins and fairies and elves love to play,
Live all the dragons. Yes, dragons, okay?

They fly through the skies, they dive, and they dip,
They loop and they swoop, they flip and they skip,
If ever you see one, then oh, what a sight,
As they soar through the air to the highest of heights.

There goes one now, and boy, she flies fast!
The trees sway and swoosh as she hurries on past.
Where is she off to? A flash and she's gone.
Waking the sun with his big yellow yawn.

But not every dragon is up yet today,
And this lot are only now rising to play,
They must be the funniest dragons in Quace!
Did I mention that Quace is the name of this place?

The littlest dragon is called Baby-Boo,
She's cute as a button and only just two,
She jumps up and down in her favorite spot,
Which is on top of Daddy and not where she ought.

Now poor Daddy dragon was loving his dream,
Of eating plum-cakes topped with dollops of cream,
But now he's awake and he's coughing up flame,
Because Baby-Boo's bouncing, yes, she is to blame!

Her brothers awoke and they looked all around,
Then they rushed to find out what was making this sound,
Frederick and Yederick were their first names,
They got up to mischief when not playing games,
Their sister was bouncing, and Daddy looked sad,
They laughed when he coughed, "No, it isn't that bad..."

Breakfast time next, Daddy cooked up some grumpkins,
He spread them with groobles, and pumpkins and lumpkins,
Mommy left early; she was off to a meeting,
Daddy sat down and the kids started eating.

This wasn't so bad, he thought, calming his fears,
But Frederick and Yederick had other ideas,
They both spread their grumpkins with snooze-berry jam,
And when dad turned his head, they both threw them.
Splat! Wham!

Their Dad was not glad to be sticky and red,
"What's going on? We are just out of bed."
But he cleaned up the mess and as soon as he had,
The children went right back to acting all bad.

Dad thought 'twould be easy, to care for his young,
But by 10:36, well, the fun had begun,
Their kitchen, once clean, was now chaos and clutter,
And who was that cat that was covered in butter?

That cat was not their cat, oh no he was not,
And the butter was melting because it was hot!
Dad cleaned up some more, but by 1:24
Every toy in the house had been thrown on the floor.

His kids were not dressed yet, they needed a wash,
He looked at their faces and thought, "Oh my gosh!"
"Boys run and play while I bathe Baby-Boo,
Just wait your turn and then you can splash too."

But the boys couldn't wait, and the walls looked so white,
They got out their brushes and painted them right,
But no paint did they use on them, no paint at all,
Those were blueberries splattered all over the walls!

The house was a mess like an earthquake had hit,
"Let's go out," Dad said, "please, just for a bit."
The sun was a-shining, and the birds were a-chirping,
Yederick was slurping, and Frederick was burping

"Go off and play nicely," said Dad with a roar,
What harm could they do, he thought, here out of doors?
The twins smiled sweetly and said, "We'll be good!"
So, Dad felt quite glad that they had understood.

But in less than an hour, the grass had been charred,
And somehow some cows were now roaming the yard,
The flowers had vanished, the gate was now gone,
Dad just shook his head and thought "What have they done?"

The house was all messed up with mud and with muck,
And inside the shed was a big clucking duck,
And up in the tree why, a truck had got stuck,
And it seemed to be burning, his children had struck!

He sent off the children to fly and to roam,
He had to clean up before mother came home.

Dad gathered his tools to make everything right,
He called up his friends and he mustered his might,
The clock was against him; there was so little time,
To clean up the mud and the grumpkins and slime.

And that's when he saw it, its tail aflame!
Down from the sky, a big asteroid came,
Towards his three children there right in its way,
He took to the sky for he must save the day.

The asteroid blazed as it raced through the air,
The dragon flew harder, he had to get there,
Then, at last, the kids saw it but saw it too late!
No time to escape, from their fiery fate!

It was almost upon them when Dad roared their names,
And 1,2,3,4 times he shot it with flames,
Two blasts of yellows, then orange and red,
He blew up that asteroid over their heads.

The pieces rained down, the children all cried,
Mama had looked on with fear in her eyes,
She flew to her family, her kids had been saved,
By her husband so loving. A father so brave.

Frederick and Yederick said, "Mommy, we're sorry!
We've been really bad and caused Dad lots of worry,
He saved us and that's made us see what we've done.
We'll never again wreck the house having fun."

Their parents both smiled, just glad all was right,
But Daddy remembered the house was a sight,
"We'd better go home now, but I must confess:
There is a small chance that there might be a mess."

Try to find 8 differences.

Thank you for reading!

I hope you enjoyed this cute little story.

If you have a chance, I would appreciate you writing a review and share your experience. This valuable feedback will allow me to write my books better and better. So let me know what you are thinking about.

Thank you in advance for helping me out!

Marie Blair.

Made in the USA
San Bernardino, CA
25 August 2019